SOP 3

KU-545-655

RESTORATION COMEDY

Adapted by Maureen Spurgeon from
original Cosgrove Hall Productions
script by Jimmy Hibbert
and directed by Chris Randall.

CARNIVAL

Carnival
An imprint of the Children's Division
of the Collins Publishing Group
8 Grafton Street, London W1X 3LA

Published by Carnival 1988

Count Duckula is a registered trademark of
THAMES TELEVISION plc.
Copyright © COSGROVE HALL PRODUCTIONS 1987

ISBN 0 00 194472 X

Printed & bound in Great Britain by
PURNELL BOOK PRODUCTION LIMITED
A MEMBER OF BPCC plc

Transylvania . . . A place where the sun never shines, the air is filled with evil and terror . . . Here stands Castle Duckula, home for centuries to the most terrible of vampire ducks. Blood-curdling screams echo from the very depths of its midst . . .

"Aaaagh! Aaaagh!" Count Duckula was having another nightmare. "Aaaagh! Nanny, Nanny!"

The whole bedroom shook. There was a deafening crash of bricks and stone, and an enormous hole gaped in the wall. It was Nanny, of course.

"Whatever's the matter, Duckyboos?" she cooed, reaching out with her good arm.

"I-I've had the most horrible dream, Nanny, and – and . . ." He pointed a trembling finger at a sinister shadow coming towards him. "W-who's that?"

"Only Mister Igor, bringing your breakfast!"

"Breakfast!" screeched Duckula. "I won't be able to eat a thing! Th-that dream . . ." he stammered. "I-I dreamt I was eating a giant hamburger – huge, and – and meaty, and . . . Oh, no! Where's my pillow? Don't say I've eaten my pillow!"

"It's on the floor, Milord . . ." said Igor, stooping down. "It must have fallen off the bed!"

"Whew!" Duckula was most relieved. "Thank goodness!"

"N-not that particular word, Sir!" Igor shuddered. "Please . . ."

"Which word, Igor? Goodness?"

"Urgghgh! Yes, Sir! If you could avoid using it, Sir . . ."

"Igor," said Duckula, "you're always looking on the black side! Still," he considered, "living in this dump is bound to make you depressed, the huge, crumbling, out-dated monstrosity!"

"Now then, young master," Nanny quavered. "That's no way to talk about your old Nanny!"

"Not you, Nanny!" Duckula snapped impatiently. "Duckula Castle! What this place needs is cheering up! Some colour and a bit of life!"

"Milord, please!" begged Igor, deeply shocked. "No more of such talk!"

"My mind is made up!" insisted Count Duckula, sticking out his yellow beak most determinedly. "There's going to be some changes around here!"

And before either of them could open their mouths again, he had vanished, re-appearing next minute inside his very own vampire telephone booth!

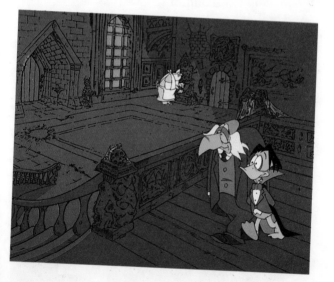

"Hello? Is that the Transylvanian Morning Sun? I'd like to put an advertisement in your paper!"

It so happened that someone else was very interested in the Transylvanian Morning Sun. In fact, Doctor Von Goosewing read it at breakfast every morning, before he started on the important task of vampire hunting.

"*Wally the friendly werewolf needs a home* . . ." he read aloud, and gave a snort of disgust. "Such rubbish! Whoever heard of a friendly werewolf?" He read a little further, his coal-dust eyes glinting behind his spectacles.

"What's this? *Interior Designer wanted to decorate Transylvanian Castle . . . Applications to Count Duckula, Castle Duckula, Transylvania Avenue, Transylvania . . .* Hmmm . . ."

And at that very moment, back at Castle Duckula, there came a loud knocking at the front door.

"I'll get it!" came Nanny's wavering voice –
followed by the usual bangs and crashes of bricks and
timber smashing down to the floor.

"Now . . ." pondered Nanny, looking blankly at a
piece of door in her flabby hand. "How did that
happen?"

"It matters not!" a dramatic voice declared, and a
tall lean figure in a big, floppy hat, big, floppy bow
tie, and a pink waistcoat stepped daintily into the hall.
"The moment I saw it, that door said: Keep Out!"

"Oooh!" exclaimed Nanny. "It never did!"

"What we want it to say," the visitor continued with
a wave of his long, thin arms, "is Come In!"

"Ah, Count Duckula, I presume!" he continued, holding out his hand. "Allow me to present my card!"

"Mr. Roberto!" read Duckula, most impressed. "Designer to the stars!"

"I am he! And the moment I saw your advertisement in the Transylvanian Morning Sun, I said to myself: Roberto, I said – that job is you, you, you!"

"Men!" he called out, with an elegant clap of his hands, and two workmen in overalls shuffled forwards.

"How do . . ." greeted one.

"Morning . . ." said the other.

"Ah, good!" cried Duckula, pleased to see something happening. "Shall I show you around?"

And without another word, he ushered Roberto towards the hall – leaving Igor and Nanny to retreat into the kitchen.

"I don't like that Mister Roberto!" Nanny confided, all three chins wobbling at once. "If he doesn't go, then I will!"

"I have a better idea, Nanny!" said Igor. "We shall go on strike! Refuse to do any work!"

"But, who's going to make his broccoli sandwiches?" gasped Nanny. "Who's going to read him his bedtime stories?"

"Nobody, Nanny!" Igor insisted impatiently. "No one is going to make his dinner, or iron his shirts, either!"

Had he known what was in store, maybe Duckula would not have been quite so pleased about showing Roberto around . . .

"This hall says Mirrors!" he was saying. "Mirrors from ceiling to floor! Make a note of that, men!"

He turned to Count Duckula.

"And now," he said grandly, "to the basement!"

"Oh, you mean the dungeons . . ." Duckula corrected him without thinking. "Oh – er, I-I mean . . ." he giggled nervously, "the cellar. That's it – the cellar!"

"Call it what you will!" declared Roberto, as Duckula began leading the way down a flight of stone steps. "It will become a transformation of gleaming gold and tinkling chimes . . . A pleasure dome of delights!"

"Wow!" breathed Duckula. "I think it's time for a snack!"

He began making his way towards the kitchen, hands behind his back, and looking every inch the master of Castle Duckula.

"Nanny! Nanny!" There was no answer. So Duckula tried again, louder this time. "Igor! Hey, Igor!"

He was amazed to find them relaxing in the kitchen, Igor dozing with the newspaper over his face and Nanny humming to herself, knitting needles clicking away merrily.

"Ah, there you are!" cried Duckula. "I was calling for you at the top of my voice!"

"That's right, dear," agreed Nanny, without looking up from her knitting. "Quite a lot of noise you was making, too!"

"A remarkable pair of lungs you have," added Igor, briefly removing the paper from his face. "If I may be so bold."

"What?" Duckula stormed. "So, why didn't you answer?"

"Because we're on strike!" informed Igor.

"On strike?"

"Precisely, Sir . . ." said Igor.

"But, I'm hungry!" wailed Duckula. "What's all this about?"

"It's about that dreadful man, Mr. Roberto!" Igor enlightened him. "Nanny and I will not lift a finger until he goes!"

"Mr. Roberto?" echoed Duckula. "He's gone!"

"Oh, well . . ." breathed Nanny, making a beeline for the refrigerator. "In that case . . ."

"But he's coming back tomorrow!" finished Duckula triumphantly. He wasn't too pleased when Igor went back to sleep and Nanny's needles started clicking away once again.

"All right!" he thundered. "Have it your own way! I'll just have to hire someone else, that's all."

And soon, he was making another telephone call . . .

"Transylvanian Morning Sun? Oh, good! I'd like to put another advertisement in your paper . . ."

And – guess who was reading that very same paper the very next morning . . .

"Wally the werewolf eats old lady who offers home . . ." mumbled Von Goosewing, viewing the headlines with much distaste. "Well! Didn't I say there is no such werewolf as a friendly one . . ."

"Hamburgers und frankfurters! What is this?" He traced along the page with a trembling forefinger. "Butler und Housekeeper required? No previous experience necessary! Must be good at snacks! Apply to Count Duckula, Castle Duckula, Transylvanian Avenue, Transylvania . . . Zo!" He jumped up in excitement. "Count Duckula, your days are numbered!"

And soon, he was knocking at the door of Castle Duckula, dressed in a rather peculiar way . . .

Meanwhile, Count Duckula was waking up as usual. Screaming out, as usual. Sitting up in bed – as usual. But when Nanny did not appear, as usual, to bring him his breakfast, as usual, he remembered about the strike.

He was just getting out of bed ready to go and fetch something to eat, when there came a series of thundering knocks at the front door.

"Igor!" yelled Count Duckula without thinking, and then remembered about the strike again.

"Oh!" he puffed impatiently. "This is so inconvenient! Looks like I'll have to answer it, myself!"

He marched angrily along the hall, stamping so hard that each footstep made the window panes rattle.

But Doctor Von Goosewing, standing on the
doorstep, didn't hear a sound. He was much too busy
thinking how clever he was in his butler-and-
housekeeper disguise, lifting one scrawny hand to
knock at the door a second time.

"Yes?" snarled Duckula, now in a thoroughly bad
temper, and yanking back the door so hard and so
suddenly, that Von Goosewing was left still hanging
on to the door knocker!

"That's funny . . ." muttered Duckula, looking all
around. "I could have sworn I heard someone
knocking . . ."

"Ja, ja!" bellowed Von Goosewing from the
direction of the door knocker. "It was me!"

"What?" shrieked Duckula, spinning around in some alarm. "You nearly made me jump out of my feathers! What's the idea, sneaking up on me like that?"

"But," explained Goosewing, "I have come in answer to your advertisement in the Transylvanian Morning Sun!"

"What?" Duckula shrieked again. "Then there's not a moment to lose!"

He helped Goosewing down from the door knocker as fast as he could.

"To the kitchen!" he cried. "I need breakfast – and quick!"

"Zo!" responded Goosewing "I am hired?"

"Oh, yes, Mr. Hired!" said Duckula enthusiastically. "I should say so!"

Meanwhile, Mr. Roberto and his two workmen, Norm and Den, had also arrived at Castle Duckula.

"To work, my good men!" Mr. Roberto commanded them, with an airy wave of his hand. "Work hard! Work with care! But, above all," he finished, with a dramatic pause, "work with love!" And, with the utmost care, he unfolded a large sheet of paper. "Here are the plans!"

And Roberto was not the only one with plans that morning . . . As it happened, Von Goosewing had already started work . . .

"Count Duckula!" he called towards the dining room. "How do you like your stake?"

"Steak?" repeated Duckula, not understanding what Goosewing meant. "Steak? I thought I told you I was a vegetarian!"

A low, strangled cry made him whirl around in his chair. "I might have guessed!" he spat out. "Goosewing!"

"Ach, you monster!" yelled Von Goosewing, lunging towards Duckula with a wooden stake. "You haff seen through mine disguise, ja?"

Duckula managed to shrink back just in time, only seconds before Von Goosewing plunged the stake right into the breakfast table, making the crockery wobble most alarmingly.

"On second thoughts," he yelled, deciding to make his escape through the front door. "I think I'll skip breakfast!"

But Von Goosewing was not the sort of vampire catcher to be beaten that easily . . .

By this time, Roberto's workmen, Norm and Den, had set up the scaffolding, and were having a break, sitting together on a convenient plank and enjoying a nice cup of tea. Duckula could see them through one of the upstairs windows.

"Hey!" he yelled out. "Do you know you've blocked the front door with your scaffolding?"

"Yeah?" queried Den, without much interest.

"Yes!" shouted Duckula. "So, you'd better unblock it! And, quick!"

Norm and Den each drew in a deep breath.

"Can't do that, guv!" Norm told him. "It's our tea break, see? You'll have to wait till we've finished!"

"Can't promise nothing, mind," added Den, just to be on the safe side.

Duckula was absolutely furious. He scrambled out of the window, stomping along the planks on top of the scaffolding.

"Strikes!" he snarled to himself. "Tea breaks! And I still haven't had my breakfast! Now – how do I get to the kitchen?"

And, as Count Duckula began storming in one direction, Norm and Den at last put down their tea cups and started walking along in the other . . . almost bumping into a very strange-looking man in overalls around the next corner!

"Ah, zo!" greeted Von Goosewing, in his usual bumbling way. "Guten morning! I am ze new workman, come to assist you!"

"Mister Roberto didn't say anything about no new workman . . ." said Dennis.

"Mr. Roberto! Ja! He said to tell you that he didn't say anything, because he . . . because . . ." Von Goosewing thought desperately for a moment. "Because – he is forgetting!"

"Oh!" grinned Den, and tipped his bowler hat. "Right!"

"That'll be it, then!" said Norm.

"Fooling these two dim-wits was almost too simple . . ." murmured Von Goosewing under his breath. "Now Duckula, you villain – your end is at hand!"

"You can start work by getting that scaffolding away from the door!" Norm told him.

"And we'll be putting the kettle on for our tea break!" finished Den.

"Ja . . ." agreed Von Goosewing, watching them slouch away with mounting excitement. "Tea break . . . . of course . . . Hah! Now I will find Duckula and blast him off ze face of ze earth!"

He began tip-toeing along the scaffolding planks, squinting painfully through the dusty spectacles perched on the end of his crooked nose. Next minute, the air was torn apart by a piercing cry . . .

"Aaaagh!" shrieked Duckula, still trying to find his way back to the kitchen. "Goosewing!"

"Zo, Duckula!" Goosewing snarled back, pulling out his stake-firing gun from inside his jacket. "You haff seen through mine disguise again!"

"Aaaagh!" Count Duckula screamed again, fleeing for safety around the nearest corner – and passing Norm and Den, who were once more sitting side by side and quite enjoying another nice, peaceful cup of tea . . .

"I'm going to get you, now, you blood-sucking monster!" screeched Von Goosewing, taking aim with his gun.

"Only one thing for it!" puffed Duckula, quite out of breath. "I – I'll have to jump!"

Once again, he was only just in time. The very next instant, Von Goosewing had shot the stake through the air – and into a scaffolding pole, sending Norm and Den plummeting to the ground. Not that this stopped them enjoying their tea!

But Von Goosewing was not so lucky. Piece by piece, the rest of the scaffolding collapsed at an alarming rate from beneath his flapping feet!

"Help, help!" he bellowed in his cracked voice. "I am falling!"

And so he was – with whole piles of planks and poles tumbling down on top of him. Duckula couldn't help feeling pleased that he had taken that jump and missed the entire avalanche!

It was then that Mr. Roberto arrived on the scene, completely ignoring all the signs of chaos and confusion around him.

"Ah, there you are men!" he greeted Norm and Den. "And how is the work getting on?"

"Well," said Norm slowly. "We got the scaffolding up . . ."

"Scaffolding?" repeated Mr. Roberto, a trifle frostily. "Scaffolding? But – why?"

"Well . . ." said Den. "We always puts scaffolding up! Don't we, Norm?"

"But I am an Interior Designer!" Mr. Roberto felt bound to point out. "*Interior!* I have no need of scaffolding!"

"Well, that's all right, then," Norm assured him. "That new bloke got it down again!"

"New bloke?" Mr. Roberto could hardly believe his ears.

"Yeah!" Den nodded. "The new bloke you sent!"

"But – but . . ." Roberto faltered helplessly. "I sent no one!"

"Well, that's all right, then!" said Norm again, quite unperturbed. "'Cos he's gorn!"

"Please," begged Mr. Roberto. "Please, no more! My head spins! I can see that I shall have to do this job, myself! To work, men!"

By this time, Nanny and Igor had decided that they'd had enough. For hours on end, there had been nothing but banging and hammering, and shouts of "To you, Norm!" and "Left hand down a bit, Den!" with dust flying about, and dirt and mess everywhere.

"Our strike is not working, Nanny," Igor pointed out. "Something must be done!"

"Yes, Mister Igor . . ."

"This cannot go on any longer!"

"No."

"We shall have to take matters into our own hands!"

"Yes!"

"Roberto will have to go!"

"No, Mi--- Er, I mean, yes . . . No! Oooh! You've got me all of a muddle now, Mister Igor!"

"Oh, do listen, Nanny!" pleaded Igor wearily. "I have a plan to get rid of that dreadful man, once and for all. Here's what we do . . ."

Roberto, of course, suspected nothing. In any case, he was much too proud and pleased with himself to notice anything at all unusual as he prepared to show Count Duckula the results of his design work, conducting him grandly towards the great hall.

"My hall of mirrors!" he announced airily, waving a limp hand towards the rows of mirrors along either wall, and pausing to admire his own reflection. "Mirrors impart such a feeling of . . . of . . ."

He stopped re-arranging his bow tie, looking around desperately for some reflection of Count Duckula.

"Is something the matter?" Duckula enquired. "You've gone kind of pale!"

"Wh – where are you?" stammered Roberto. "Wh-where's your reflection?"

"Oh, don't worry about that!" said Duckula. "Look in a mirror, and there I am – not there! Runs in my family!"

"Vampire!" screamed Mr. Roberto, backing away hurriedly. "Vampire! Help!"

"Aw, come on!" pleaded Duckula, holding out his two yellow hands. "I'm a vegetarian! The very thought of blood---"

Mr. Roberto gave an even louder yell.

"Blood? Eeek! N-no! Keep that beak away from my neck! Help!"

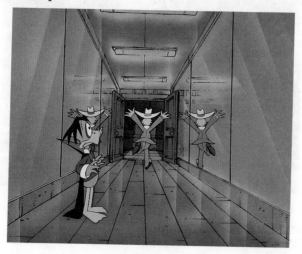

"Hey, come back!" bellowed Duckula, beginning to run after him, and bumping into Nanny. She appeared to have her hands full, towing a small cannon, Igor following close behind with a lighted taper . . .

"Oooh, Duckyboos!" she squealed, quite concerned. "Did Nanny hurt you?"

"N-no . . . I'm all right . . ." He paused, a somewhat puzzled expression clouding his face. "Hey, Igor . . . Nanny . . . What are you doing with that cannon?"

"We – we were, er---" Igor hastily put the lighted taper behind his back. "We were polishing it, Sir!"

"We seen that Mister Roberto come past just now," commented Nanny, changing the subject. "Gorn, has he?"

"Yes, Nanny, I'm afraid he has."

"And them nasty workmen, too?"

"I suppose so . . ."

Nanny heaved a sigh of relief. "Oh, good!" she said.

"Does that mean you're not on strike any more?" Count Duckula asked eagerly. "Can I have my breakfast now? Please?"

"Of course!" cooed Nanny. "I'll get it right . . . Ooops-a-daisy!" Nanny never could go far without bumping into something or someone! This time, it was Igor.

"Nanny!" he cried, struggling to keep his balance.
"You clumsy . . ."

He wobbled precariously, then toppled towards the
ground, putting one hand out to save himself.

Such a pity it happened to be the hand holding the
taper, all ready to light the fuse of the cannon . . .

The bang resounded through the whole of
Transylvania, shattering Von Goosewing's vampire-
catching nerves, and sending a fresh supply of shivers
through Mr. Roberto's sensitive frame.

"Gosh!" breathed Duckula at last. "That scared
me!"

"Still, we'll clear up the mess later, after I've had my
breakfast! Or, is it lunch by now? I'm so hungry, I
think I'll have both!"

"Oh, dear . . ." quavered a voice.

"What is it, Nanny?"

"Oh, Duckyboos . . ." It seemed that she hardly knew what to say. "Mister Igor's shot the kitchen!"

There was a whole minute's silence. Then Count Duckula let out an ear-splitting yell.

"Oh, no! My breakfast! My lunch! Aaaaagh . . .!"

And so, once more, blood-curdling screams echoed through Castle Duckula. Once more, mournful wails began drifting towards the tall, menacing peaks of the Transylvanian Alps.

Because, once more, things were back to normal for Nanny, Igor, and that fearful monster, latest in a long line of evil vampires – Count Duckula!